it's hard to say

claire hopple

word west press | brooklyn, new york

isbn: 978-1-7369477-5-3

published by word west in brooklyn, ny

first us edition 2021

printed in the usa

www.wordwest.co

cover & interior design: word west

for Grandma

table of contents

To:

"& if not for our small / rituals / how would we get
out / of the house"
— Hanif Abdurraqib

chapter 1

tate

To my coworker, Tate—

On the edge of the parking lot, where it meets the road, Google Street View caught me in the midst of an offense.

To be fair, this was the same morning a homing pigeon had dropped out of the sky and into the husk of seagrass in my backyard. A message had unfurled from its right leg as it shuddered away a life beside my slippered feet.

The message said: WORK HARD. THEN WORK HARDER.

I thought, this is the cause of all our trouble.

I thought, this message probably killed its messenger, strung out on finding its way home. What kind of home it must have been.

I had to leave the pigeon where it was without a proper ceremony or I would've been late to work. Like I wasn't even heeding its cautionary tale whatsoever.

Nobody'd seen what I did to you once I showed up to work, hunkered and sinister between the company's allocated spaces, so I thought I was in the clear. Encumbered only by remorse, I settled in and trawled my desk drawers for emergency chocolate.

And yet here I sit, weeks afterward, across from Janine of all people, in the only barren office, waiting to hear how much she already knows.

"Here it comes," I accidentally say out loud.

I could say I had no idea what I was doing that day, that I was utterly confounded, stuck in a morning haze or struck by an external zomboid force too powerful to shake off. But glancing at that screenshot she had taken the liberty of printing out, I look like a person who knows exactly what she is doing.

Janine is scratching her head and I'm scratching my head and I don't know who started it, who's mimicking who.

I never learned how to moonwalk but right now I wish Michael Jackson's ghost would float in and show me how to glide gracefully back in time. But he doesn't appear so I look for more papers underneath the screenshot, perhaps filled with exculpatory testaments to my pristine employee record. There's just that one sheet on the table, though.

Janine's not speaking and I remember she's watched a lot of those CSI series, the ones that have aired so long they need colons with extra acronyms beside them to tell them apart.

"Sure, he ratted me out for leaving at 4:45 a few Fridays ago but I'm over that."

I am now wading in her embarrassment for me. "Tate loves to snowboard. His custom licenseplate says so," she taps the picture, "You knew that." Angie-from-IT's face looms in the door crack. Her expression could be interpreted as having eavesdropped on the entire conversation.

Janine is taking the high ground. She's restrained.

The taste of my own medicine is like broth. It is a base for something much richer. It knows its place and strives to be even blander.

Sure, you, the victim, are technically my subordinate. But it really only worked out that way on paper. You are younger yet more mature. You have what can only be described as poise, a word I understand in the abstract but can never manage to pull down into self-application.

Before you came on board, we were unified in our quiet sterility. The overhead lights left us overexposed and stupefied into slothlike submission. In other words, we were always finding new ways to let our work curdle. We were proud that a company as small as ours had an entire floor to itself in a mid-century office park too far back from the main drag to get a good look at.

Then people started clotting around your desk, not even on our end of the hallway to see you. Everyone took to you within the week. You initiated Capture the Flag nights on Tuesdays. You convinced Bill to try squid at the holiday party. Before I knew what had happened I'd gone through my senior solo dance routine from high school for you in our galley kitchen.

You told me that secret about Lauren I'd never heard despite the fact that Lauren and I are a two-person department. I dog-sat for her and made her mother a casserole when they had a death in the family.

You watch movies on your computer in segments throughout the day and when you noticed that I'd noticed you laughed and said, "Computers," while shaking your head like that would fix it. I didn't respond, so maybe that did fix it.

I guess what I'm most repulsed by is my own interest. And that repulsion led me to do what I did, which was dump Bill's cologne down through your open sunroof until it puddled up on your bucket seats and seethed in your power window buttons.

And as Janine pulls on the door handle of her makeshift interrogation room precisely the same way she pulls on the basement vending machine to release her Snackwell's Vanilla Creme Sandwich Cookies, I think maybe I have learned from this experience. How we're not as invisible as we think we are, if nothing else.

Instead of going directly back to my desk I meander to the supply closet and check the shelf with the lost and found bin. I pocket the TI-83 calculator circa 2002 to relieve the pressure of the situation and leave the pamphlet about hand, foot, and mouth disease behind.

The HR report will be there or not there on Monday. This report will eventually make its way into the filing cabinets that are never opened, or it won't make it there at all.

chapter 2

sophia

To my childhood best friend, Sophia—
He seems unaware that he is being watched. The bathroom door is cracked enough for me to see him, whether I want to or not. I am on a plane but we haven't gone anywhere yet.

You would think he looks unexceptional, especially from this narrow vantage. He is fully dressed and might be tucking in his shirt but still has his puffy coat on. I think I see something—a weapon? a knife?—stashed in the back of his pants. But then really I can't see much of anything.

If I did alert an attendant, what would I say? That I was peeping on a man in the bathroom and he may or may not be trying to kill us all? If he is a killer, he must not be a very good one. He can't even shut doors completely.

I hear running water. I back up but I'm already against the side of the plane. His secret is disguised under tepid fashion. I can't look when he steps out. I can't even try to go to the bathroom anymore. Panic has evaporated the liquid straight from my bladder.

Along rows of seats speckled with lives, I head back, duped into following passenger protocol. My senses bloat and I hear what can only be the crepitations of a Cheeto bag behind me.

If anything really is happening, I just want it to be over.

I find my headphones and set the white noise to "Airplane Cabin" while in the airplane cabin but am not ready to find this funny.

One of the flight attendants goes into his spiel and I can just barely make it out. When he gets to the part about not smoking on the plane he throws me a surly expression, like I'd be the most likely culprit. I don't know why I'm not worthy of respect just because the air vents are reddening my eyes.

Holding a magazine seems like the thing to do. Let's see, should I read about an inheritance dispute that ended in a family member getting murdered due to a clerical error? Or how about a woman who was accidentally kidnapped and her life was changed for the better?

The overpriced bottle of water can no longer hold its condensation and reanimates a channel on the magazine cover left by a previous spill.

I guess I should mention that I'm flying to visit you. I should also mention that I brought my sick cactus and am cradling it in my lap. Maybe I should have qualms about being a cactus lady on a plane but I can't seem to muster them. Since you claim to be an amateur horticulturalist maybe you can tell me what to do about these pinkish brown spots that have developed.

We aren't close anymore. You know I have a bad habit of not thinking about important people and then when I do see them I'm instantly crushed by all the missing I was supposed to be doing the whole time.

It's easy to blame distance but that only has so much to do with it. I often feel closest to you when I'm alone and especially distant from you when we're together.

I guess this moment would also be a good time to mention that what was originally supposed to be my special trademark is becoming a compulsion. Rummaging through every lost and found I encounter has transformed me.

I've started cataloging noteworthy items. One page looks like this, for example:

Oakley Library Lost & Found Contents

Lantern
Elvis shot glass
One maraca
Putt-putt score card (partially filled in) Rutabaga, whole

I once found a noose. Well, I guess it could have been a regular rope tied up as a macabre joke. There's a storm way out there. Or it's heat lightning, which is really just all of the passion and none of the warning.

It may be hot out there but it is cold in here, and so I fish a knit cap out of my bag, an original from the lost and found closet (yes, they have a whole closet) at the Y. When I put this on, I become the owner. This person manages a teenage punk band named Courtesy Flush and has at least two boxes of fish sticks in his freezer. He takes it upon himself to tell everyone he knows about the latest recalls. From canned goods to laptop batteries, he will keep you in the loop as long as you're still fogging up the glass beside him.

I always wait to be invited to your house. I never intrude like this. And yet here I am.

Last year, when you asked, you said, "I already know you're not busy."

I hadn't even answered the question yet.

It's true that I believe people only become parents to have something over on somebody. I find it difficult to trust parents and non-parents who think they know what's best for everyone, since I've always hurt people the most when I'm trying my hardest to prevent it, and some of my most vengeful acts have actually improved the lives of my enemies. And that I frequent the dog park but cannot bring myself to own a dog. That my last date was with a significantly older man who kept saying, "You know, I was 16 once," repeatedly throughout dinner. And also that if you were here, you'd use this deboarding lag time to pull a Zimbardo and recreate the Stanford prison experiment with fellow passengers while I can only manage to stare and blink.

But still, what a thing for you to say.

chapter 3

teryn

To my restaurant server—your name tag says you're Teryn—

My friend Nicole isn't allowed inside the tavern anymore, so this time, I go alone.

She'd already been on thin ice with the management since inciting a few riots in there, but when she camped out in the parking lot for 48 hours, that really put them over the edge.

She had been staking out her own parents at the time.

Nicole knew her mother was hiding something when she found her literally hiding something. The last time Nicole had stopped by, her mother was burying what looked like old photographs in the backyard.

The tension between her parents had ripened. They'd

both been runaways with patchy backgrounds. Her father had once been Furniture King of Toledo. He now made a living constructing apparatus for furniture that had uneven legs, and furniture that existed in spaces with uneven floors. There's a lot of imbalance to profit from.

Spackled with self-doubt, I stutter along the vinyl, failing in my attempt at a graceful slide into the booth.

You are my server and you will be taking care of me this evening. And you know the specials.

When you come back for my order, right before you take the menu, you let it slip, "I want to kill my neighbor's dog."

You laugh, then continue, "Is that harsh? I've always thought of myself as an animal lover, but... it's not even a bark, it's like, like this screeching..."

You walk away before finishing your sentence.

"What is the meaning of this?" I say to you but you are already a few tables over.

I don't know if that confession is your way of revealing something to a stranger to safely release it, like a balloon with a message to a dead person inside being lifted into the sky, or if this is your attempt at a contract of closeness, a relationship initiation. This approach can't possibly help with earning tips.

I build a mental scaffolding of potential confessions to reciprocate while awaiting my soup and sandwich combo plate.

1) This is the year I live on Butt St. So basically it's an unmarked road. Any time a new street sign goes up the teenagers bound over with freshly minted permits to disassemble it and commandeer it within the week. They keep wrenches in their glove compartments for this express purpose.

2) I wake up with commonplace existential dread. All the who-am-I-how-did-I-get-here thoughts jack-olantering me in the early morning that's really still night.

But looking in the bathroom mirror fully awake in the daylight I'll feel it more intensely. The white towel behind me is a sheeted ghost, the only one sure of its costume.

I learned that surface skin cells last about a month. Thousands of these cells are crumbling away from us every hour, totaling around a million per day. So those trite questions seem legitimate. We're completely different humans at this point. Meanwhile, our former cells/selves are tangled in carpets, caught in the woodgrain of tables, coating the threads of our beflowered blouses.

3) Even with all of that mirror-gazing, I know my coworker Tate's face better than I know my own.

4) Since my only adult friend living in the same town as me—yes, the one who's no longer welcome in this establishment—heard about my lost and found documentation project, she let me loose in the back office of the hotel she manages.

Nicole explained that they try to keep a handwritten log of items and bag them with labels that display room numbers and dates. But sometimes they get angsty or bored or busy and they shove them in abandoned food service boxes.

She also told me that some guests left behind a player piano once. It was before her time there but the veterans still talk about it. No one's sure how they got the thing up to their room undetected, especially since it didn't fit in the elevator.

And not only did she let me rummage around in there for close to an hour—when I discovered the lone

steering wheel, I strained not to find metaphorical—
she also let me pick something out for my collection.

5) I selected a jar of tonsils that I've since carried with
me everywhere. I draw a kind of ceremonial strength
from them. They must be in our bodies for a reason.

6) This project might be my pitiful attempt at collect-
ing life. I refuse to think about whether that's true. We
can't take it with us but we sure do try.

Enough already.

"Was that guy really bragging about not having
been to the dentist in 30 years?"

You ask this while slapping down the check in its
polite little holder. I want to weigh in, but I wasn't there.

The pen seems to deliberately roll away from me as
I reach to sign.

We both ignore a scream coming from the bar.

"If you do end up murdering the dog, I'll raise
funds for your attorney fees. I'll have a bake sale," I say.

You punch me on the shoulder in hypothetical
gratitude.

You leave me to figure out your cut of the bill. I
imagine sending you postcards in prison with images
of skydivers or airplanes or cruise ships on the fronts to
rattle your inertia.

The customer copy reads COME BACK AND
SEE US and I vow that I will try my best.

chapter 4

nicole

To my conveniently located friend, Nicole—

We agree to liaise at the apartment building. I picture myself shepherding you through the tour and already feel perturbed before I've parked.

We surveille the vestibule and await developments. You hang your arms over the railing and momentarily drop your head.

"This cruelty-free deodorant has turned out to be anything but," you say.

This three-story brick complex is barbarous and listless enough to suit you. A distant television is the only sound. There are bike tire tracks on the walls opposite the mailboxes. All the trappings of a dwelling you would consider renting. Or at least looting.

The landlord or property manager or whoever arrives. She sedates us with small talk and you politely avert your eyes.

Her precious schoolmarm demeanor has little effect on me and it's difficult to determine whether I should be proud of this.

She leads us up to the third floor.

"This dining nook is large enough to host a dinner party, if I can muster enough friends to appear," you notice once we're inside.

She runs through the floor plan and the numbers with you while I test the plumbing. I go to wash my hands but can't figure out how to turn on the sink. I pull at things and twist certain parts but nothing budges. I look underneath it, on its sides, flip the wall switches just to be sure. I walk out and remain quiet.

The woman gets a phone call.

"How's school?" I ask.

You look startled.

"Let's find somewhere we can discuss this." I oblige.

We move into a bedroom.

"First of all, your enthusiasm is becoming a problem. If you must know, school is going okay. I have this...semi-respected professor who's very complimentary of my work. But it seems as if he's becoming senile so I can't really take him seriously. I have to question all of it."

The woman ends the call and joins us, walks to the far side of the room to open a window. While she's leaning to lift it, you focus on my face and whisper "defenestration" like you want me to push her out into the gravel lot below.

"That abandoned car in the ravine down there should be towed by next week," she says as she turns around.

She gets another call. I wonder if she is some kind of real estate magnate.

"And are your parents still in that, uh, rough patch?" I squint at you.

You tell me about running into your dad at the grocery store and him not recognizing you. How he blamed it on your wearing a hat. That he disclosed he'd kept a secret pet hidden in the garage. Your mom unearthed the ferret behind the bucket of badminton equipment and later hissed at your dad when he attempted to recuse himself. Then how your mother retaliated by purchasing a used lifeguard chair from the Internet and planting it in their pool-less backyard to survey the neighborhood and whistleblow at behaviors she observed but didn't take to.

"Melodrama" sounds more like a caramel-based candy bar than the highly emotive scenes it contains, though I think both are equally fabricated.

When we've seen everything there is to see, you shake her hand while saying, "Please accept this symbolic gesture. Remember, the name's Nicole."

I glance back to observe her wiping the hand she shook with on her skirt. She probably didn't mean for me to see that.

I pick up what looks to be a Girl Scout badge from the grass. According to me, this counts as a lost and found item, though technically there isn't a box or designated area involved. The badge was lost and I just found it.

You sum things up by saying you haven't been too pleased with your own behavior lately, and so, acting as the only adult in your household, you have grounded yourself.

"It's customary to stay home unless there are prearranged appointments such as these."

You are learning that adulthood is basically a series of deciding things but never really getting to decide anything at all.

You've probably made it back by now and are reheating a bowl of some leguminous dish in your microwave.

I didn't get a chance to tell you about the trap door at work. The door leads to what may or may not have once been a cellar. Employees regularly submerge their senses there after talking to clients (and each other) all day. The place seems ideal for a cigarette break, but no one smokes, so we end up bringing down lukewarm LaCroixs and standing around with those.

There isn't a trap door anywhere in my house but I wanted a similar environment so I've created what might be a sensory deprivation closet. There's nobody to escape from in this setting—only myself, and that is plenty.

You probably wouldn't have a clue what to make of this news anyway, and you're an adult who's grounded herself, so what do you know?

chapter 5

hank

To my former neighbor, Hank—
The fastest recorded escape from a straight jacket while underwater is 22.86 seconds. I'd like to say I still remember that from when you told me. When your voice became flatter and more hollow like it was trying to escape from its own straight jacket. But I had to look it up.

It's noble you tried for that Guinness record for however many years and just got really close. Though I don't know if or how you get over such a thing.

There's some hubbub at the block party across the street. A movie scene or, perhaps more accurately, a prescription drug commercial is developing. People are talking and laughing and loping across the lawn in full sun with an otherworldly ease. Their fluidity looks simple and pure. It seems like something I should be able to do.

I'm playing back the last voicemail I have from you

as a pathetic talisman for summoning the courage to make my way over there with all the neighbors.

"...People have pelted me with a power washer before and they probably will again..."

Ah, yes, this was part of your defense. A few of the neighbors I'm seeing over-gesticulate to one another at the block party right now had once accused you of some light arson, if you recall. Simply because you seemed capable. Well, that and you'd thrown all your valuables into the Sikorskys' pool well before the flames reached your weeping cherry tree.

You had what could only be called a reputation. Once a few of us had learned about your traumatic brain injury from an accident that may or may not have been someone attempting to murder you, and that the injury had led to scientists studying you—well, we didn't really know what to do with that.

Which was why we just went along with it when you started throwing food from your porch at some of the teenagers. You kept saying it was a food fight but the throwing was one-directional.

Even though you've been gone for two years, some neighborhood kids are still afraid of you. Nobody has ever been afraid of me.

You threw me off a bit too the first time I saw you. Beside a giant, unbridled mutt, you emerged from your garage wearing a tie covered in tiny Tabasco bottles. I smirk when I think about your dog, Bartles, how you rescued it from a sorority house and the girls had already named it after their favorite brand of wine cooler.

"...Don't lie to me with any nonsense about a lawsuit because I already know you don't think Justin is going to pass the bar exam..."

Your voice had a haughtiness that came from living

on this street the longest. Though that isn't the case anymore, I guess.

You are somewhere in Minnesota right now. A woman has replaced you. Why she's here doesn't add up. But that is a different story.

Her first day in, she started a property line controversy. She didn't appear to notice the death stares as she staked little neon flags where she thought they belonged.

I've always felt that I am both too good and not good enough for your friendship. Like, I can picture you sitting on my porch but I can't imagine you on my couch.

I've started pilfering from local lost and found boxes and making it into this whole project. Recently, I've been labeling all the items with a label maker. Labeling them not what they are but who they belong to. By that I mean whose face claims my mental real estate when I pick up an item or merely spot it from another side of the room.

The Bob Ross Chia Pet I excavated from Claxton Elementary displays your name across the bridge of Bob's nose. Who will commandeer the actual kitchen sink from the bus station is to be determined. They say "everything but the kitchen sink," but let me tell you. I already told you. The things people leave behind.

The end of your message cuts in and out, but I hear you mention something about my inability to endure eye contact and I swear you said the phrase "Pen Pals" but I might be making that part up.

Are you still a window washer or did you trade out your life completely?

Okay, it's pretty obvious I'm hiding from them. I am sitting and deciding what I've already decided. I'm closing most of the blinds so they think I'm out, possibly at a different party.

This isn't part of your message of course but I can

hear you telling me there's no reason to avoid them. You'd be saying, "It's exactly like in the movies. It's really as easy as it looks. It's not only a matter of time—it's a matter of space, too. And it's nothing. It's not really anything at all."

chapter 6

stranger

To a total stranger, whatever your name may be—
I take things personally like anyone else, including the quote on my chocolate wrapper.

"Today is a bubble bath day," the foil tells me. Its triumphal sparkle does not help.

I'm supposed to be meeting Nicole at the town carnival. But her cancellation text appears and congeals to my mood as I enter the premises, dismantling my developing ring toss strategy.

She is supposedly conducting a last-minute interview with a gentleman from the Internet. She has a penchant for peeping toms. She hires them to watch her through her bedroom window. The things people will do for a decent night's sleep.

A tornado came through last night but never touched down. Still, the high winds had harvested mangled clumps of debris and a nimbus of collective anxiety.

I spy a field trip permission slip in a divot and hope that this boy Asa made it onto the bus before it puttered over to the science museum.

Maybe it's just as well that Nicole couldn't be here. I planned on confronting her about unapologetically dating a guy in the animal testing department of a popular makeup brand. They use hamsters. So I guess things could be worse.

I don't know who else to invite. The number of available people is dwindling. I try not to read into it. I don't really have what it takes, anyway: the overwhelming sense of guilt endemic to friendship.

As the crowd expands to the size of my interpersonal limitations, you bump into me. You hit right into the talismanic jar of tonsils at my side, nestled in my bag, which collides with my hip bone and most definitely leaves a bruise.

Lowing in moderate discomfort, I'm distracted, but I think I can identify you among the townsfolk. They're the same faces pretty much every day, but they all have different ways of ignoring each other. Your face is new.

I forgo the funnel cake and decide to chase you. You couldn't have gone far.

I pass those partial mannequins in a shop window downtown. The severed torsos next to the crotches-with-legs.

Is that you down the hill with your buddies?

The tollbooth attendant at the corner parking garage might lead me to the right place. I could question the parkers inside to see if they know you. They can navigate tight turns and breathe easily under low ceilings while straining to keep pressing engagements. What can't they do?

Okay, I guess this is happening. I approach the guy

behind the glass box in the garage. He has a clipboard. He is clearly in charge. He has a pen too. Looks like a felt tip.

Of course, a clipboard can belong to anyone. I know that. They're not just for the responsible. I've grown to respect those who can go places and complete ordinary tasks, seemingly without incident. This may have something to do with feeling like I'll spend the rest of my existence doing penance for my brief stint as a child.

I'm swallowing excessively.

"They're doing big things with pens these days," I say to him.

He looks up.

I make like I'm trying to pay for parking, but I'm still on foot. My mode of transportation has not changed.

I flee, then return to the fluorescent field. Nicole's here. She's lying on the hay bale in front of the spinny ride. She's prone. She's prone to lying prone, on bales across the country.

"There you are."

"He was a no-show," she says, swinging her leg. She stands, stretches. I wonder if I should recommend you for the job.

We linger at a kiddie pool filled with rubber ducks. Nicole promises to win me an oversized alligator.

"If you run into my dad, avoid saying the word 'umbrella' at all costs. In fact, never speak the word in his presence. I'll explain later."

I temper my curiosity. "Can you hold a seance for a living person?"

"Definitely not."

You may be thinking: It was just a bump. These things happen in crowds. Why am I searching for you?

These are understandable thoughts.

Recently, I inherited my aunt's house. She died a while ago, but nobody felt like doing much at first. My family consented to moving me in while passively avoiding any removal of her possessions.

Steeped in her belongings, I fear I'm slowly becoming her.

Even the fragments that remain—crumbs in the little drawer under the stove, runes of nail holes and scuff marks on walls—exert their influence.

Could a house be considered one large lost and found?

We circle the horde of bicycle cops. Two teenagers make out on a bench. Tractor engines and generators pummel our ear canals.

Then there's our catching up, Nicole's embellished tales, my shrugging off of coworkers in shorts emerging from the Ferris wheel line, her craving for foods impaled by sticks, and our eventual dissolving into the night.

I have yet to see that oversized alligator.

chapter 7

Rhea

To my sister, Rhea—

I'm convinced I met your imaginary friend. He was exactly as you described. He's my neighbor now, I guess.

Our aunt lived a couple hundred yards from a serpentarium, so since I've inherited the property, I live a couple hundred yards from a serpentarium. This thought can instantly embroil my mood depending on the circumstances.

I used to think I was becoming our Aunt Trish, glomming onto her belongings and glutting myself with the vestiges of her existence. Lately, though, it's more like I'm turning into the house itself. My joints synch with the walls in their wee-hour cracking, for one. The sole feature of the yard is a privacy screen of trees, for another.

This guy—you used to call him Jerry, but the real

person's name is Ames—when I first located him, he was scrounging around my driveway. He looked to be pointing at and measuring the air around my truck.

Up until that juncture, I hadn't met any of the neighbors. The house across the street appeared unoccupied save for the porch with its piles of junk and a radio playing at all times, seemingly unattended.

After scribbling some figures in a notepad and collapsing his measuring tape, he rapped on the door.

He locked eyes with me and went in for a handshake with both hands.

"Your truck is the ideal size for a casket." These were the first words he spoke to me. His stalagmite nose hairs were longer than his stalactite nose hairs.

I was made privy to the situation: He needed to bury his cousin in a prearranged plot the next state over. His transportation was unfit for duty.

If I were a different kind of person I would have asked more questions.

And unlike you, I'm not often needed, and have long since fallen out of practice.

Instead of figuring out my response, I was wondering why hands are always folded in caskets. Are they waiting for us to leave them alone, to get to the resting in peace part? Or for us to finally 'fess up?

Then I was watching him back out of my driveway to pick up said cousin, tapping my mailbox just a little with my tailgate on the way out.

Ames insists on running the headlights in the daytime like a funeral procession. He claims innumerable construction zones and preexisting traffic violations as reasons.

Yes, I am going with him to deliver the body. After watching him leave for the pickup, I had just enough sense not to let him cross state lines by himself with the vehicle, but also not enough sense to not let him cross state lines by himself with the vehicle. I've nestled in as a participant in the process.

I'm avoiding another favor by going along. Nicole recently asked if I could talk some sense into her father. Her parents are in the midst of some marital strife. Her father has been hiding out in a movie theater as of late for close to a week. Reportedly slinking from one showing to the next in the inviting darkness, though mostly hovering in the vicinity of any drama so he could hear an actor bawling on screen instead of doing it himself. As their adult child, Nicole thinks it's a futile pursuit for her to intervene.

Instead, I'm learning about Ames' wife. She sells her wares in a vestibule at the mall. She makes customized memorabilia, like a family photo infused on a mousepad, for example. I neglect to point out that mousepads may or may not have been rendered completely useless at this point in history. She always smells like Auntie Anne's. Occasionally a whiff of that new clothing smell from those fast-fashion places intermingles. She hears the prodding bass from those very stores in her sleep. All of this, according to Ames.

One son is a foosball champion and the other son is experimenting with puppeteering.

"But these days, our Yorkie is the baby," he says while hunkering down to excavate his bag of sunflower seeds.

I'll later find a single seed on the carpet and add it to my collection for that project I was telling you about.

As you know, I don't put on a voice when talking to babies, or puppies for that matter. I talk to them in the same voice I use on adults. You also know how unsettling this can be in certain crowds.

Phil Collins sings us a tale about his easy lover. Ames starts to drum the beat but loses interest after the first refrain.

Like Jerry, or Ames, or whatever you want to call him, you haven't been real for many years. You are a previous self, one selected from a series of selves and clutched as if realer than your others. But then I think people are constantly acting out their truest selves and that I am constantly reacting to a fluid scene. Like I don't really have a choice. This I accept unquestioningly, letting the notion drag me into the Earth's inner core, aflame with misperception.

We enter a tunnel and strive to maintain speed. The orange squares lining the walls shine down on us in the truck's cabin, making us downright holographic.

chapter 8

mom and dad

To my parents, Sue and Jeff—

Never mind where we are going and what we are transporting across state lines. Ames will meet his family at a certain location later on today. He's the one who lives beside Aunt Trish's house, though I guess it's my house now.

"These moments will last forever and it's all your fault," I say to him.

Ames insisted we stop at a public park in the middle of the day for a bathroom break during our road trip.

The park's facilities are all locked up for the day. We checked. But he really can't wait.

Everyone else has already relinquished their prime frisbee knolls or their partially deflated tennis balls and left for home. Wasps colonize their sticky remainders.

Ames would go first and I would be the lookout. Leering into tinted windows and watching my back—these were things I could do.

It's my turn now and right as I'm scavenging for a shaded alcove, a voice calls out rather performatively, I think.

"You can't be doing that here."

A woman in khaki shorts, hands on hips, is picnicking on my premeditated malfeasance.

I can picture your expressions. You shouldn't be surprised by any of this. Your rule-following natures were Rhea's birthright, not mine, and you both know it.

I'm able to hold it like a respectable person. Ames points to a gas station with a Subway inside. "Go there and lunch is on me. I haven't paid for a sub from that chain in over two years. We have an arrangement. Paperwork has been drawn up."

It is hard to tell whether he is more proud of himself for the free subs or the paper trail.

We get lost on the way to our ultimate destination and end up meandering through clovers of suburban cul-de-sacs. A Cozy Coupe idles in a driveway with freehand flames painted on its doors.

Someone has left a pile of discarded belongings on the curb. Ames' hand eclipses my view in his exasperated gesturing. He wants me to pull over. He must search through it.

Before I know it I'm dusting off a solitary, fugitive shoulder pad as Ames clasps a pool noodle. He scours the landscape, plucking out a thick sweater clotted with knots of thread.

He slips the sweater over his head in the car to try it on and a glimmer emanates from his neckline. I follow the chain to its logical conclusion and think I see a lump of metal in the shape of...a locket? A locket like the kind kids used to wear with inexpertly lopped pictures of family members or true loves inside them.

I didn't notice amid the mural of junk, but somehow he's pulled on roller skates and laced them. They mostly fit but his toes are scrunched enough to form distinct outlines.

Who am I to balk at a trove of curbside artifacts, though, really?

We strain to find the right road once again. We approach a quaint town square with a fountain in its center. Inside the fountain, a woman howls, arms windmilling splashes, while the carved figure beside her looks askance in patinaed shame.

We finally find the place we're looking for and get ready to drop off what we're supposed to. I stay in the car.

Ames approaches the door and I hear a man say something like, "We were not aware of a deposit today. Nobody contacted us."

Ames rambles, his voice climbing in volume and picking up speed like a train.

The man matches his tone, shouts something about an appointment.

Ames flails but loses ground. He tries to stay defiant as he roller skates away.

He gets back in my truck and starts rifling through the interior for some reason. Maybe to calm his nerves. Two lists of directions emerge. These two lists are ancient, and you each wrote one, back when you thought I needed help getting home from college. One of you wrote out the route with less mileage that took a couple minutes longer and one of you handled the route with more mileage that was slightly faster. The handwriting and descriptions are each distinctly yours. They're both only about a sheet and a half's worth in length but they are vast. They are stories. They live in the middle console, and they've lasted beyond the GPS, though you can still see the circle on the windshield where the suction cup used to be. They've made it past a couple of phones that told me where to go after that. And if I'm smart, they'll make it past the brain that tells me how to use all these directions to get to these places. Regardless, they'll definitely outlive this truck.

Once he's calm, I guide him through putting everything back in the right order.

"What's with the locket?" I ask.

An ice cream truck beckons in reply from some unseen avenue.

"It belonged to my sister," He says after a considerable pause.

He goes on. He grew up with twin sisters. When they were teenagers, they used to take long walks down the main drag together. After months, maybe years of this practice, one of them jumped in front of a bus. And the other, within seconds, followed. They weren't upset or suicidal. The family didn't understand. The jumper was badly maimed and pulled through. The follower did not. Through testing and interviews they were able to mostly sort things out.

"Folie à deux," Ames says.

"What?"

"Shared psychosis. Nothing could be done. No one to blame. Couldn't be helped."

He seems unaffected, his voice neutral. I guess this was a long time ago.

There's not much you can say to a person after that. And we still have the package we were supposed to deliver sliding around in the truck bed.

I know we'll eventually return home even though I can't picture how. We'll yell back and forth at each other from our stoops unnecessarily loudly, not for a wider audience but in mutual pretending that our houses are further apart than they really are, which is close enough to lob a bagel from one kitchen to the next. We'll get there. It'll be sooner than we know.

chapter 9

me

Notes to self—

I will meet a taxidermist named Christopher at a party on Haywood where he is getting baptized in a hot tub wearing aggressively neon swim trunks. We will date. He'll understand shoving life back into something that has already left.

We'll slip out together to have a conversation on the lawn and I'll think I hear "That's not a good idea" coming from someone nearby, but disentangling the source will prove impossible. Any one of them would have said it to my face.

I'll remove the singing electronic trout mounted to Aunt Trish's wall right before he comes over for the first time. This will be the same night he tells me about the bird sneaking into his workshop and falling in love with one of its stuffed counterparts. Instead of romantic, this story will seem menacing.

He will bleach skulls, then cut our sandwiches into manageable triangles. I'll consider moving on with a man who owns a salvage yard for the sake of something new while sticking to my sensibilities.

He will preserve. And still, I won't be able to keep straight the difference between preserves and jams and jellies and marmalades.

Clamped into cuddling, I'll confess that my secret ambition is to live inside a word problem. How many apples will I have left in my cart? Tell me, grade schoolers of America. Show me with your numbers.

Christopher can cut straight with scissors (the first of his kind I will ever meet), even in this moment, before I know him.

Despite his profession, mortality will continue to baffle me. I'll blame old movies with actors dancing, eyes begemmed with vigor, of trying to think of where (or what) they are now.

I'll need to break into my own house at some point while he is with me.

"Fake it 'til you make it, make it or break it, break it if you bought it," he'll say unhelpfully while I'm funneling myself through a window.

This house is built on a sinkhole, which my mother already told me, but I frequently and conveniently forget. It sinks about an inch per year, or so I was told. Maybe I'll be like a captain going down with it. Our spines make staccatoed question marks while we wait.

There are many closets to spelunk, and eventually I'll unearth a Dairy Queen cake book from the back of the pantry. Whether Aunt Trish once worked at a DQ or stole this book outright will remain a mystery. The layered birthday cake with the clown face might have buoyed her straight through the 1990s. But then again, maybe buttercream doesn't hold that kind of power.

I'll also retrieve a globe marked with places that no longer exist from a basement filing cabinet and fondle Yugoslavia on one of many Tuna Casserole Thursdays. Christopher will ruin another one of these Thursdays by becoming a mustachioed acrobat, maneuvering his way out of our arrangement by declaring vaguely that he must save the rainforest.

I will send him off with waves fit for a teen pageant. I will mean business.

I'll mistakenly think I'm afraid of the near future when I'm actually afraid of the distant past.

Some people won't return those few letters I've actually sent, even when I politely ask for them back. No matter. I'll forage for the ones that have never left my possession. I'll consider burning them in avoidance of a posterity that will never arise. Instead, I'll take them away from here. I will carry you all on my back.

previously published

Chapter 1 was originally published in *Hobart* as "The Messenger."
Chapter 4 was originally published in *Okay Donkey* as "Now We're Getting Somewhere."
Chapter 5 was originally published in *Vol. 1 Brooklyn* as "It's Hard to Say."
Chapter 6 was originally published in *No Contact* as "Don't Mention It."

acknowledgments

Thanks to my family and friends who have stuck around even though I'm allergic to phone calls.

Thanks to my lit community, especially Mallory Smart, Nick Gregorio, Kevin Sampsell, Jan Stinchcomb, Justin Souther, Crow Jonah Norlander, Jennifer Greidus, Christina Rosso-Schneider, and others who tolerate my replies to their tweets.

Major thanks to David Byron Queen, Joshua D. Graber, and the word west team for accepting this book and making it better.

And John Harlan Hopple, my forever-first-reader and chef.